Destroy Malevol

'A plan is only as good as those who see it through.'

Malevolence, the gigantic Separatist battleship, is under attack by Jedi Cruisers led by Anakin Skywalker. With his ship's ion cannons destroyed and its hyperdrive disabled, General Grievous seems to have no escape.

But Count Dooku has a plan. "Do not compound your failure this day by allowing our prize warship to fall! Heading towards you is a very important Galactic Senator. With her as your hostage, they will call off their attack."

On their way to attend secret negotiations with the Banking Clan, Padmé and C-3PO drop their ship out of hyperspace.

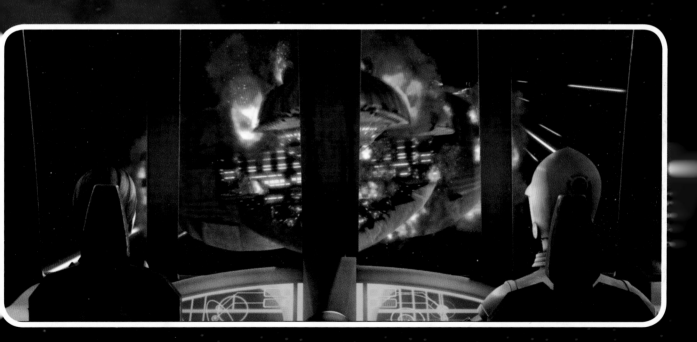

"This isn't right. That's a droid warship! We're in the middle of a battle!" says Padmé.

As Padmé manoeuvres to avoid laser-fire, her ship is picked up on the *Resolute*'s scanner. "Master, I'm picking up a signal near the enemy vessel! Something just came out of hyperspace!" Ahsoka reports.

At the same time, on the bridge of the *Malevolence*, Grievous smiles. "Good. Our hostage has arrived."

"I believe the Jedi are attempting to contact us," says C-3PO with relief. But Anakin's warning to flee comes too late! Grievous activates the tractor beam and Padmé's ship is pulled inside the *Malevolence*'s hangar bay.

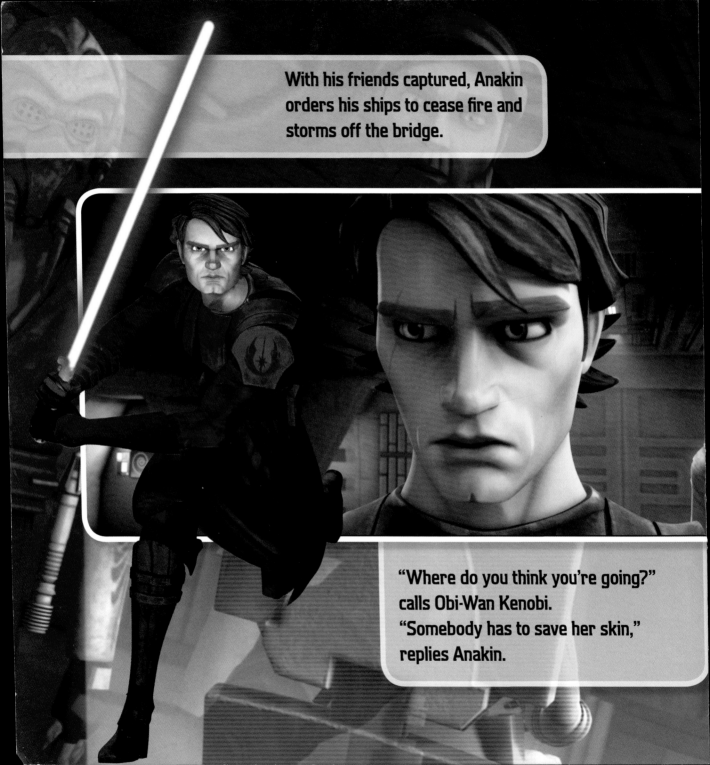

With his friends captured, Anakin orders his ships to cease fire and storms off the bridge.

"Where do you think you're going?" calls Obi-Wan Kenobi.
"Somebody has to save her skin," replies Anakin.

Padmé, realizing they're trapped, busies herself at the controls. "Come on, I've just overloaded the power system," she tells C-3PO.

While battle droids cover their main exit, Padmé and C-3PO sneak out the lower doors of the ship and make their way out of the hangar.

Grievous strides confidently onto Padmé's ship but notices the cockpit controls blinking a warning.
"Looks like the engines are set to destroy themselves!" says a battle droid.

KABOOOOM! The blast throws Grievous clear of the fireball that engulfs the ship.
"Sound the alarm – we have stowaways on board!"

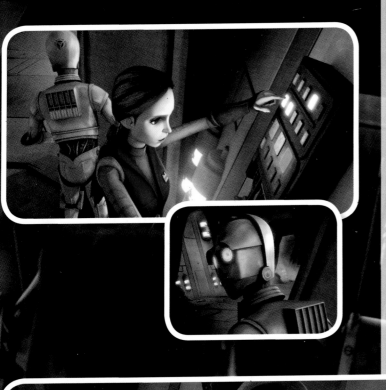

Padmé and C-3PO, trying to use the *Malevolence*'s comm to contact the fleet, overhear Grievous and his battle droids searching for them. Quickly hiding themselves, they also overhear a battle droid's report:

"The damage to the hyperdrive was not as bad as we first thought. We should be able to get underway again shortly."

Evading its scanners, Anakin and Obi-Wan dock on the *Malevolence*'s emergency airlock and have to act fast to avoid capture by some passing droids!

"You stay here, Artoo," says Anakin. Beeping dutifully, R2-D2 takes up his position as lookout.

On the bridge of the Jedi Cruiser, Plo Koon and Ahsoka are organizing back-up when a transmission comes through from Padmé. Ahsoka quickly patches it through to Anakin's comlink and plans are made to rendezvous.

But on the bridge of the *Malevolence*, Grievous intercepts the transmission and hatches his own plan . . .

The rendezvous point is a busy multi-level junction where jet cars on rails criss-cross in every direction! Dodging battle droid fire while leaping from one jet car to another, Anakin rescues Padmé. But C-3PO is scooped up by a speeding car in mid-jump!

"Blast! That's not good," growls Obi-Wan, as he watches the droid disappear into a tunnel.

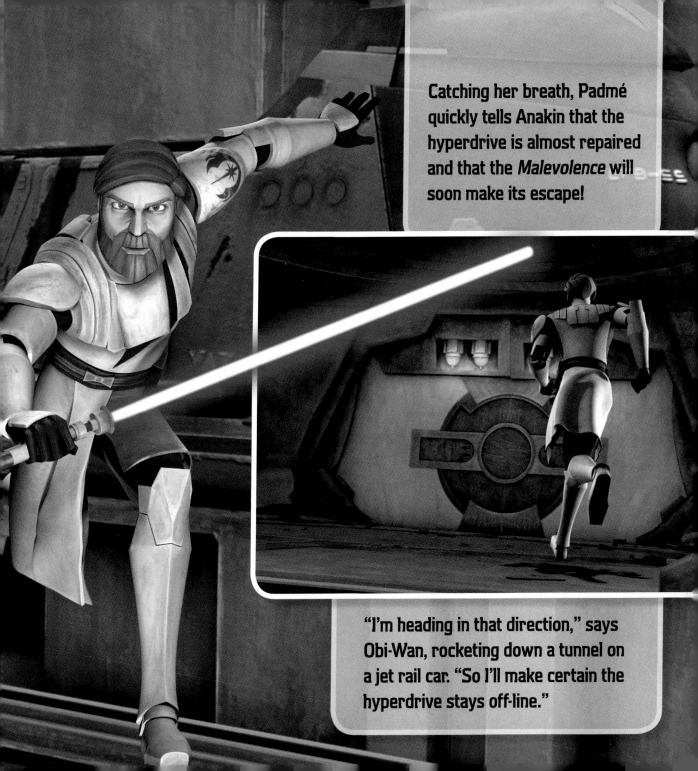

Catching her breath, Padmé quickly tells Anakin that the hyperdrive is almost repaired and that the *Malevolence* will soon make its escape!

"I'm heading in that direction," says Obi-Wan, rocketing down a tunnel on a jet rail car. "So I'll make certain the hyperdrive stays off-line."

Anakin uses his comlink to contact R2-D2. "Artoo? I need you to help me find Threepio."

While R2 jacks into the *Malevolence*'s computer port, Obi-Wan whizzes towards its engine rooms to sabotage the hyperdrive – only to find Grievous and his guards waiting for him.

"Hello there," laughs Grievous evilly.

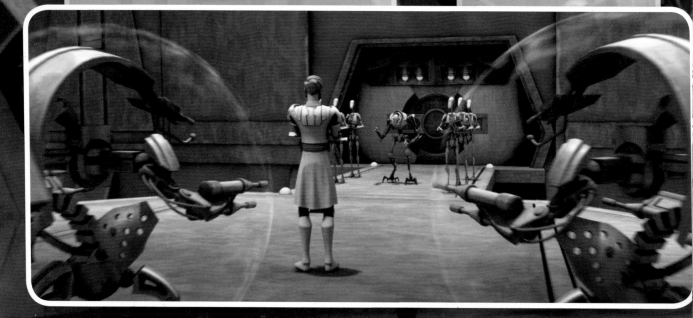

But killing Obi-Wan Kenobi was never going to be easy! By using the Force and a series of expert rolls, Obi-Wan escapes the engine room, with Grievous in pursuit.

"Guard the hyperdrive! I will deal with the Jedi myself!" he snarls, storming after the retreating Jedi.

With his plans changed, Obi-Wan calls Anakin. "We'll rendezvous back at the *Twilight* . . ." he starts to say before his comlink is jammed by the *Malevolence*.

"We have to do something!" yells Padmé over the noise of droid fire. "Follow me," smiles Anakin.

Wandering down a corridor in another part of the ship, C-3PO is scared.
"Oh, lost in enemy territory. This is terrible!" Suddenly he hears familiar burbles and squeaks.

"Artoo-Detoo!" he calls happily. "Oh, you're a sight for short circuits!"

On the bridge of the *Malevolence*, the doors of the turbolift SWISH open and Anakin jumps out, lightsaber flashing! With a few practised strokes, the danger is neutralized and he marches over to the navicomputer.

"I'm going to hot-wire this ship – give Grievous a little surprise," he says.

Meanwhile, down in the jet rail tunnels, Grievous is gaining on Obi-Wan. It is only by the Jedi's grace and skill that he makes his escape! As he speeds off in the opposite direction, Obi-Wan gives Grievous a little salute . . .

Anakin finishes tweaking the navicomputer, as Padmé hides the last pieces of smashed droid and they flee the bridge. Moments later, the battle droid captain and pilot return.

"Repairs are finished. Prepare to charge up the hyperdrive," says the captain. Below them the turbolift doors open and Anakin and Padmé meet up with C-3PO and R2, with Obi-Wan arriving seconds later!

ack onboard the *Twilight*,
bi-Wan contacts the
Resolute to let them know
hey're safe and clear of
he *Malevolence*.

"All batteries, open fire!" Plo
Koon orders. But Grievous, in
his starfighter, accompanied by
his vulture droids, is in pursuit
f the *Twilight*!

From his vessel, Grievous orders the droid captain to engage the hyperdrive and retreat to friendly space. But the *Malevolence* has a big problem . . .

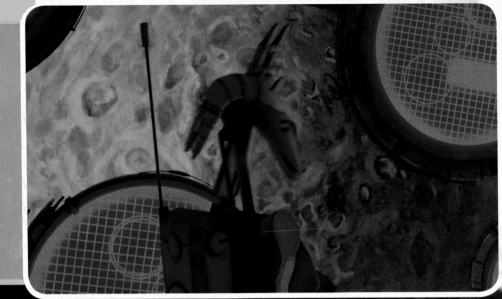

"The navicomputer is taking us right into the moon!" screams the droid pilot. With the hyperdrive activated, they don't have the time to reset the navicomputer coordinates!

KABOOOOOOOOOM! The *Malevolence* is destroyed and cheers ring from the bridges of the *Twilight* and the Jedi Cruisers!

"I imagine you had something to do with that," Obi-Wan says. "All part of the plan, Master," grins Anakin in reply.

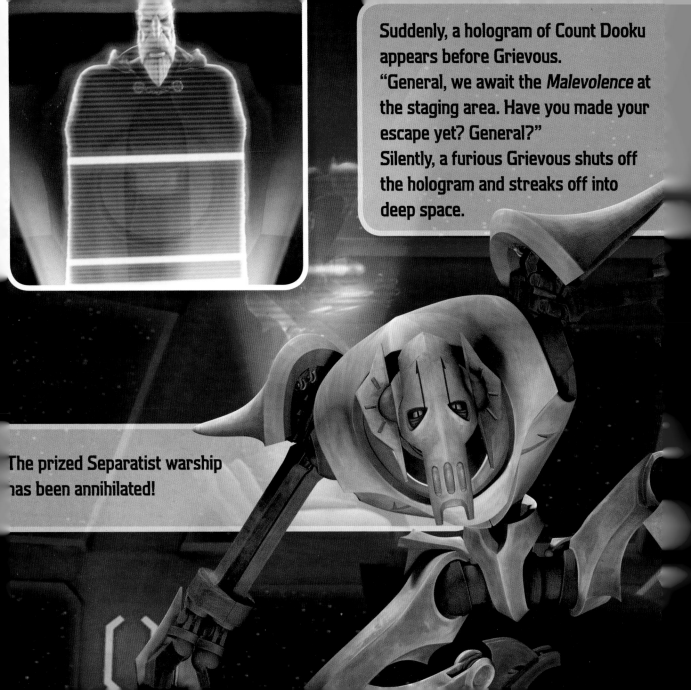

Suddenly, a hologram of Count Dooku appears before Grievous.

"General, we await the *Malevolence* at the staging area. Have you made your escape yet? General?"

Silently, a furious Grievous shuts off the hologram and streaks off into deep space.

The prized Separatist warship has been annihilated!